Wheezy the Wobbler

Wheezy the Wobbler

ISBN 978-0-9550235-6-9

Produced by
YouByYou Books,
Swallow Court,
Dashmonden Lane,
Biddenden,
Kent TN27 8BD

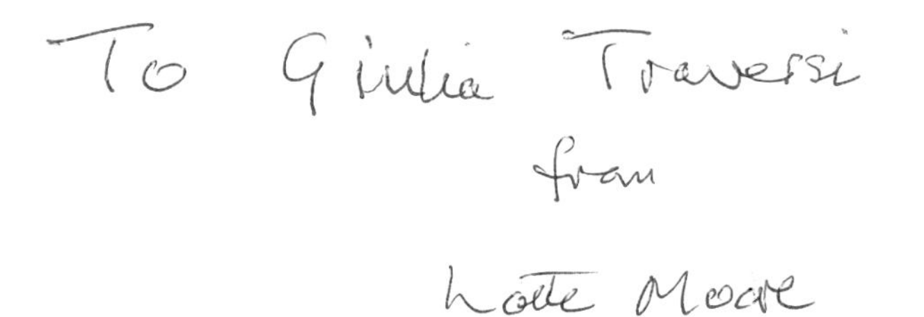

Wheezy the Wobbler

by
Lotte Moore

for my granddaughter Mimi

Waiting in the kitchen for
the children was a lovely
lime green jelly.

Mother made it for tea
and left it on the side while
she went to get them from school.

When they came back the jelly

had grown twice the size.

"What an enormous jelly you have

made for tea," said the children.

"Oh it looks so delicious,

can we have it now Mummy?"

As the children sat there

the jelly got

Bigger and Bigger.

"Oh Mummy, look it's growing".

BIS

"Well, how extraordinary",

said Mother.

"It was just an ordinary Jelly".

“ *Hmm,*” said Wheezy the Wobbler,

“I’m not a lime green jelly, I am

Wheezy the Wobbler.”

As the children watched, the jelly

plopped onto the floor.

BIS

He started wobbling

and the children laughed and laughed.

They couldn't believe it.

And as he wobbled

he moved toward the front door.

"Oh look Mummy, it's a walking jelly."

"I'm not a walking jelly,

I am Wheezy the Wobbler and

I am going to have an adventure .

... Goodbye !"...

"Did you hear that Mummy?
The jelly talked, let's go and
see what he does".

So they opened the front door
and Wheezy the Wobbler
wobbled out.

Plop,plop,plop,shake,shake

He walked along the pavement
and eventually came to a Bus Stop.

" I think I will go on the bus,"

said Wheezy the Wobbler

and so he hopped

splosh onto the Bus.

The Bus Driver
could not
believe his eyes.

"Well"
he said,

*"I've seen some things in my time
but I've never seen a jelly."*

The passengers
stared in
amazement.

*" Why are they
all looking
at me?"* said
Wheezy the Wobbler

"It's not fair....

Please, can I go to Wembley?"

"We don't go to Wembley. What's your name?"

"My name is Wheezy the Wobbler and I want to go to Wembley".

"Well you will have to change onto a number 10 bus."

"I'll go as far as you go then."

"Right, we are going to Richmond. I don't suppose that Jellies have money so you can have a free ride".

"Oh lovely," said Wheezy the Wobbler, *"I love bobbing and bumping on the bus"*.

"Next stop Richmond, you get off here".

He went plop onto the pavement.

"Umm, this is lovely fresh air;
I like this. Better than that stuffy
house we were in. I think I will go
for a little walk in the park."

He wobbled and plopped and
wobbled and plopped and eventually
he came to a lovely stretch of grass.
He rolled about in it and then saw
a steep hill *"Oh that will be fun."*

He waddled,
very slowly, puffing
a bit, up the hill. When he
got to the top he looked down
at the lovely green slope and he
rolled all the way down again....
"*Whoopee!*" he cried.

" I must go and see if there
is any water anywhere,"
so he waddled and waddled
and rolled and plopped
and shook and shook
to a little stream.

He sat down
and fell asleep under a tree.

While he was asleep some boys

came up. *“ Ha, Ha, look at this,*

a Lime Green Jelly under a tree.

A very funny looking one too,

he’s enormous,

Let’s prod him with a stick.”

"*Ouch, Ooh that hurt,*" said Wheezy the Wobbler, "*that really hurt a lot*".

“ *Oh he can talk,*” said the boys.
“*What a funny thing...Sorry, we didn’t know that you were...well, just a jelly!*”

“ *I am a jelly..*

...and you don’t prod jellies like that, it’s very unkind...I shall roll over you and make you sticky if you do that.”

"*Sorry*" said the boys and ran off.
Then a little girl came up.
"*Mummy look at this jelly, can I eat it?*"
"*You'd better not eat me,*" said
Wheezy the Wobbler, "*I'll get
stuck in your throat and hurt you.*"

"Mummy the jelly talked!" and she ran back to her mummy. *"Well"* said Wheezy the Wobbler, "I wonder what's going to happen to me now?"

Suddenly he heard something familiar; *"Whoof, Whoof, Whoof."*

"Oh no," said Wheezy the Wobbler,
"I hope that's not one of those
awful little dogs."
"Whoof, Whoof, Whoof."
"Come here" said a deep voice.
"Come along Jimbo."
"Whoof, Whoof."

And Wheezy the Wobbler heard
an awful sort of sniffing sound.
"Eeyah" he said, *"that dog's licking*
round me... and sniffing...
I hope he doesn't do anything nasty."

*"Phew,"*said
Wheezy the Wobbler,
*"I think I'd better start
moving from this funny
place. It's rather too busy."*

Just when he was about to wobble off
he heard a very kind voice;
*"What is this beautiful thing I see?
Come and look Alfredo. This is just
what I want for my shop Window."*

*"Alfredo, what do you think?
Shall we have this jelly on display
in our shop window?"*

*"What a lot of people would come
and see it and then they would
buy our lovely food."*

"*Oh,*" said Wheezy the Wobbler,
"I'm not sure about living
in a shop."

"*My goodness me,
the jelly talks!
I could have a
wonderful notice
outside saying, 'Talking Jelly
...come inside and see.'*

"*Perhaps I will become famous,*"
said Wheezy the Wobbler.

The man picked up the jelly and put it on a newspaper.
"I think we'll take this back, yes Alfredo?"

So Wheezy the Wobbler had an extraordinary journey. He was put very gently in the boot of a car.

He didn't like the car journey very much because it swayed and made him wobble even more.

"*Ouch*," he said to himself as he kept bumping into things in the boot of the car.

“ *Oh!... That’s a Wellington Boot ...*
.. that’s *very smelly,*”
said Wheezy the Wobbler.

Soon the car stopped and the man opened the door of the boot.

"Come along my little jelly, come along."

Wheezy the Wobbler was carried very carefully into a very big place which smelt of food. *"Mmm"* said Wheezy, *"just like being at home, only bigger; Lots of smells of food here."*

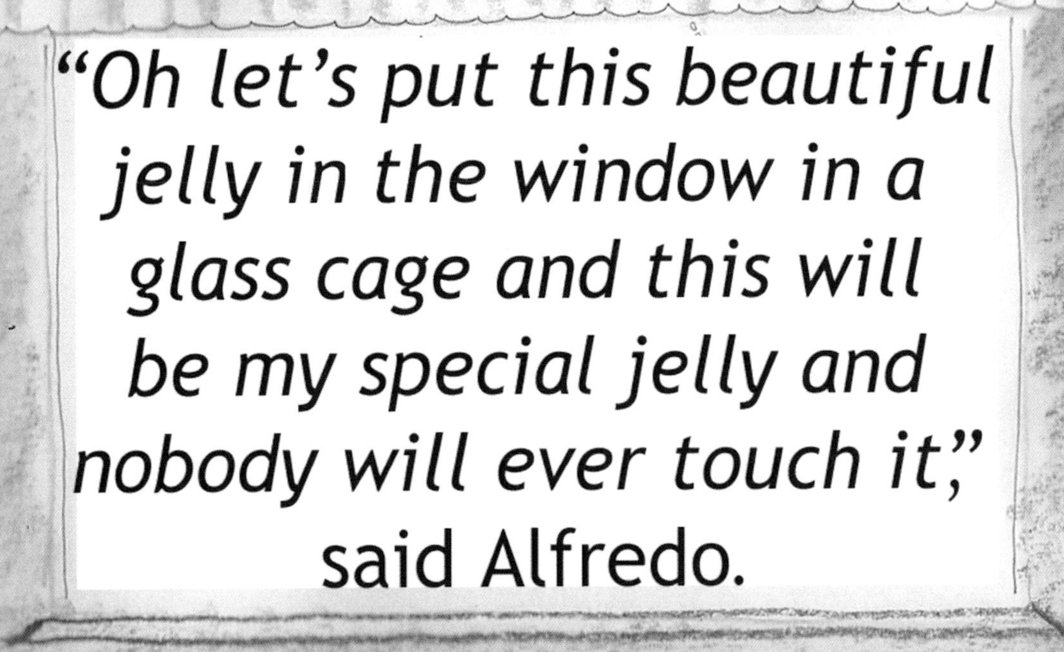

"Oh let's put this beautiful jelly in the window in a glass cage and this will be my special jelly and nobody will ever touch it," said Alfredo.

"*Oh*," squeaked Wheezy the Wobbler

"I feel great .....

I'm special at last !"

So the man put Wheezy in a most beautiful glass cage and all the people came to stare at him in the window
and they squeaked with delight .

"Look, look, look, look!"

Above the glass cage
was a notice saying

THE TALKING JELLY
DON'T EAT HIM - LOVE HIM

"*Oh*", said Wheezy Wobbler,
"*I must tell them my name.*"

So he squeaked out to all the people,

"*I am Wheezy Wobbler...*
the talking jelly.. he he he!"